The Deep Cold River Story

Written by Tabatha Southey

Illustrated by Sue Savor

Goodnight Ned, goodnight Basil.

Tabatha Southey

For Kevin Thomas.

Sue Savor

Canadian Cataloguing in Publication Data

Southey, Tabatha

The deep cold river story

ISBN 1-55263-147-8

Savor, Sue. II. Title.

PS8587.O977D43 2000   jC813'.6   C00-930771-0
PZ7.S7268De 2000

The publisher gratefully acknowledges the support of the
Canada Council for the Arts and the Ontario Arts Council for its publishing program.

We acknowledge the financial support of the Government of Canada through the Book Publishing Industry
Development Program (BPIDP) for our publishing activities.

Key Porter kids
is an imprint of
Key Porter Books Limited
70 The Esplanade
Toronto, Ontario
Canada M5E 1R2
www.keyporter.com

Design and formatting Peter Maher

Printed in Singapore
00 01 02 03 6 5 4 3 2 1

The Deep Cold River Story

ONCE UPON A TIME there was a deep, cold river

that wound its way through a sleepy little town.

It flowed along beside a park, past the fire station
and then it dipped under an old stone bridge.

It swirled over to the big city hall, past yellow houses and
near enough to the school so that the children
could see it from the playground.

In summer,
the townspeople
sailed on,
fished from
or swam in
the deep, cold river.

In winter, they would stand on the bridge,
fingers in mittens, mittens in pockets and
watch the ice jostle for space.
On the clearest days, they saw the ice
flow past the mill, meet up with the
railway tracks and run out the other
side of town.

One spring evening, just as the sun was setting, the deep, cold river paused. It stood in the middle of the town, still as a lake. Then, right before everybody's eyes, it overflowed its banks.

The deep, cold river poured down the town streets.
It scooped up the front door mats and carried them along,
bobbing them like toast in soup. People climbed up
to their roofs as the river climbed higher.

When the sun rose the next morning,
the townspeople waved to their neighbors from
their rooftops, scooped up the morning newspaper
as it floated by and read the news: "Town Floods."
They nodded wisely.

After a breakfast of wet donuts skimmed from the top of the river, they climbed in boats or onto tires and logs, dropped off their children on the roof of the school and went to work.

At work they leaned against the chimney of
the building and drank cold coffee
until it was time to go home.

EST. 1925

NED

After a week, the mayor called a meeting.

Everybody paddled to the old stone bridge to decide what should be done.

The chief of police suggested they build a dam outside the town
that would keep the water in a lake. Later, they could
build a go-cart track where the river used to run.

The fire department chief wanted to build a giant pump, pump all the water into a giant tank and then have a giant tap with a giant spout and give everyone a small bucket.

The mayor said something about a
million sponges and the high school principal
just kept shouting, "Drink! Drink!"

Finally, a little girl climbed up out of her rowboat and onto the wall of the old stone bridge. She put up her hand until everyone was quiet and then she shouted as loud as she could: "Deep, cold river—you get back in your bed!" But the deep, cold river just swirled and rushed and plunged and gushed, dodging around the houses and lapping at the branches of the trees.

The little girl tried again. This time on tiptoe

she shouted, "Deep, cold river, I said get back in your bed."

But the deep, cold river just splashed laughingly at her feet and kept on

flowing through the town. The little girl thought for a moment,

and then she sat down on the edge of the bridge.

"Deep, cold river," she coaxed,

"if you get back in your bed, I will tell you a story."

The deep, cold river paused.

All over town it became as still as a lake on a windless morning.

The townspeople held their breath.

The little girl spoke very softly now. "Deep, cold river, if you get straight

into your bed I will tell you a special story tonight and every night

for always and ever and always." The deep, cold river stood still a moment longer.

Then, with a slight, teasing ripple, it began to trickle out of the alleys until,

gathering speed, it poured out of the parks, gushed out of the trees

and quietly slipped back into its bed.

One by one, the tired townspeople got out of their boats or let go of their logs and tires and walked back to their houses.

As the sun nestled down in the sky,

the little girl dangled her legs over the edge

of the stone bridge. "Now settle down," she said.

"Are you ready? Good.

"Once upon a time there was a deep, cold river that wound its way

through a sleepy little town...."